A THOUSAND TWINKLY STARS

DAWN LESLIE &
DAPHNE ODJIG

paz publishing

Heartfelt thanks to my wonderful family, who suffers my ventures mostly gladly and sometimes sadly,
but always with love ... and to dear friends, Maureen, Candy, Denise, and Crystal,
for their unwavering support of my aspirations.

CIP-[20231002-105423]

Hardcover ISBN – 978-1-988601-33-5
Paperback ISBN – 978-1-988601-43-4
e-Book   ISBN – 978-1-988601-42-7

paz publishing

Cover and Interior Design by Alex Hennig (ClearDesign)

Printed in Canada

Additional copies of this book may be ordered by contacting:
www.pazpublishing.ca

For Tyler KT, the shiniest star in my sky.

A Bright Day Ahead, 1984

FOREWORD

Our people have been keepers of ancient knowledge. Knowledge that now more than ever must be shared.

This Pandemic was predicted by our Wise. It is known that it would be followed by a time of peace and change. We have come to many realizations during time spent alone and with loved ones. We have had the opportunity to reassess our lives. Realization of how important our families, friends and Mother Earth are to us.

What is especially profound for me is the idea TO TAKE WHAT WE NEED AND NOT MORE. As in our teachings, we were taught that everything is a circle... the Sun, the Moon, Mother Earth, the Seasons, our Lives; hence the phrase I WILL NEVER LEAVE YOU.

There is much to learn from Mother Earth if we only pay heed to her. Once we begin to understand, it is our responsibility to live by and respect those teachings. To live by example.

The children of the Earth now need reassurance and hope and this book offers some insights.

Dawn Leslie is a true visionary.

I am honoured to speak to you of my teachings and will leave you with the words from one of our great teachers, "Any decision we make must be good for seven generations, and then we will have a world for our children."

Maxine Noel (Ioyan Mani)

Maxine Noel is an internationally renowned First Nations artist of Santee Oglala heritage, and a Member of the Order of Canada. Her work has been exhibited in galleries and museums throughout Canada, and she is deeply committed to making the world a better place through the healing force of art. She signs her work with the Sioux name Ioyan Mani ("walk beyond").

But what is a virus?

she asked

Untitled, 1975

A virus is a chance,

said her grandfather

Messengers of Peace, 1991

A chance?

The Special One, 1975

It's a chance for change,

he said

Life in Harmony, 1992

But changes to what?

asked the little girl

Mother Earth Struggles for Survival, 1975

Changes

from dark to light

Voices from the Past, 1974

From wrong to right

Indian School Day, 1978

From old to new

Comforting, 1980

Each morning,
the moon sleeps so the
sun may rise and shine

Clouds of Memory, 1974

Forests burn so that tiny
trees may drink the rain
and reach the sky

From Mother Earth Flows the River of Life, 1973

Heavy snows cover the grass so that only the strongest survive

Majesty and Mystery, (undated)

And when people
lose sight of the things
that matter most

Silent Tribute, 1982

A virus is a way

for the universe to

change our path

Reflections, 1977

Families stay

nested at home

Untitled, 1986

We take what

we need and

not more

Sharing, 1979

And in serving

the whole

Cultural Identity, 1984

We grant life

to our souls

Protection, 1981

Life is a circle,

said the old man

Together, 1979

Without change,
there can be no growth

Toward a New Horizon, 1992

And every living

thing must pass

Spring, 1979

To make way

for the new

In Tune with the Infinite, 2004

Must everything change?

she cried

Moment of Commitment; 1978

Everything but love,

her grandfather said gently

Loving, 1981

Just as the moon,
who dances each
night until morning

Pow-wow Dancer, 1978

My love for you
is as bright as a
thousand twinkly stars

Enfolding, 1992

And when
I'm no longer here
to be holding your hand

Two Figures, 1980

I'll be holding on
tight to your heart.

Affection, 1978

ABOUT THE AUTHOR

Dawn Leslie is a nurse, patient safety consultant, and the author of the Healthy-Wellthy-Wise series for children, with over 150,000 books on the shelves of Canadian elementary classrooms. A self-proclaimed nomad: she's lived in four countries to date and is always up for an adventure!

Dawn is deeply committed to her wellness philosophy that children can be wonderful stewards of their own health when armed with tools in an engaging, age-appropriate format.

paz publishing

www.pazpublishing.ca

ABOUT THE ARTIST

Widely acknowledged as one of Canada's most influential artists, Daphne Odjig (1919-2016), was born on Manitoulin Island into a creative family which included her grandfather, Jonas Odjig, and father, both talented artists. While in her early twenties, she moved to Toronto with her sister, where she discovered a passion for art and taught herself to paint.

In 1972, the Winnipeg Art Gallery invited her to join artists Jackson Beardy and Alex Janvier in an exhibition called, 'Treaty Numbers 23, 287 and 1171'. The show was a sentinel event, marking the first time Indigenous artists had premiered in a Canadian public art gallery.

Shortly after, she co-founded the 'Indian Group of Seven,' more formally known as the Professional Native Indian Artist Association. The group consisted of Daphne, Eddy Cobiness, Jackson Beardy, Norval Morrisseau, Alex Janvier, Carl Ray and Joseph Sanchez, and their collective work has formed an incredible anthology of Canadian art.

Throughout a career spanning more than six decades, she explored a wide array of colours, media and styles to create a brilliant mosaic of life events, historical comments and mythological interpretations that earned her both national and international recognition. Her impressive list of accolades includes the Order of Canada, the Order of British Columbia, becoming an elected member of the Royal Canadian Academy, a National Aboriginal Achievement award,

PHOTO CREDIT - JIM JEONG

the Governor General's award, and seven honorary doctorates.

She was the first Indigenous woman artist to have a solo exhibition at the National Gallery of Canada, and in 2007, the NGC and the Art Gallery of Sudbury launched a major presentation of her work, called 'The Drawings and Paintings of Daphne Odjig: A Retrospective Exhibition'.

Deeply respected for her contributions to the First Nations art community of North America and the broader arts world, Daphne passed away in Kelowna at the age of ninety-seven.

As an extraordinary, groundbreaking Canadian icon, it is imperative that her work lives on to challenge, excite, and inspire the next generation.

www.odjig.com

ARTWORK TITLES / YEAR CREATED